# Magic
# Animal
# Rescue

Maggie and the Flying Horse

# Also by E. D. Baker

**The Tales of the Frog Princess:**
*The Frog Princess, Dragon's Breath,*
*Once Upon a Curse, No Place for Magic,*
*The Salamander Spell, The Dragon Princess,*
*Dragon Kiss, A Prince among Frogs*

*Fairy Wings*
*Fairy Lies*

**Tales of the Wide-Awake Princess:**
*The Wide-Awake Princess, Unlocking the Spell,*
*The Bravest Princess, Princess in Disguise,*
*Princess between Worlds*

*A Question of Magic*

**The Fairy-Tale Matchmaker:**
*The Fairy-Tale Matchmaker,*
*The Perfect Match, The Truest Heart*

**Magic Animal Rescue:**
*Maggie and the Wish Fish*

# Magic Animal Rescue

## Maggie and the Flying Horse

E. D. Baker

illustrated by

Lisa Manuzak

BLOOMSBURY

NEW YORK  LONDON  OXFORD  NEW DELHI  SYDNEY

First published in the United States of America in April 2017
by Bloomsbury Children's Books
www.bloomsbury.com

Bloomsbury is a registered trademark of Bloomsbury Publishing Plc

For information about permission to reproduce selections from this book, write to
Permissions, Bloomsbury Children's Books,
1385 Broadway, New York, New York 10018
Bloomsbury books may be purchased for business or promotional use.
For information on bulk purchases please contact Macmillan Corporate and
Premium Sales Department at specialmarkets@macmillan.com

Library of Congress Cataloging-in-Publication Data
Names: Baker, E. D., author. | Manuzak, Lisa, illustrator.
Title: Maggie and the flying horse / by E.D. Baker ; illustrated by Lisa Manuzak.
Description: New York : Bloomsbury, 2017. | Series: Magic animal rescue ; 1
Summary: To save an injured flying horse, eight-year-old Maggie must journey
through the Enchanted Forest, which is full of dangerous trolls and goblins,
to find a kindly stableman named Bob, who cares for many different
magical animals.
Identifiers: LCCN 2016023133 (print) | LCCN 2016049668 (e-book) |
ISBN 978-1-68119-141-6 (paperback) • ISBN 978-1-68119-312-0 (hardcover)
ISBN 978-1-68119-142-3 (e-book)
Subjects: | CYAC: Magic—Fiction. | Animals, Mythical—Fiction. |
Imaginary creatures—Fiction.
Classification: LCC PZ7.B17005 Mag 2017 (print) | LCC PZ7.B17005 (e-book) |
DDC [Fic]—dc23
LC record available at https://lccn.loc.gov/2016023133

Book design by Colleen Andrews
Typeset by Newgen Knowledge Works (P) Ltd., Chennai, India
Printed and bound in the U.S.A.
by Berryville Graphics Inc., Berryville, Virginia
2 4 6 8 10 9 7 5 3 (paperback)
2 4 6 8 10 9 7 5 3 1 (hardcover)

All papers used by Bloomsbury Publishing, Inc., are natural,
recyclable products made from wood grown in well-managed forests.
The manufacturing processes conform to the environmental
regulations of the country of origin.

*This book is dedicated to everyone who loves magic and magical creatures as much as I do.*
*And to my fans who enjoyed Bob the Stableman in the* Greater Greensward Gazette. *And to Kim, who made Bob so much fun.*

# Magic
# Animal
# Rescue

Maggie and the Flying Horse

# Chapter 1

Maggie held her breath as she watched a silver unicorn pause at the edge of the stream. He was hard to see among the leaves of the trees. A lot of people wouldn't have noticed him at all, but Maggie

was special. She often saw things that most people missed in the Enchanted Forest.

"Oh!" Maggie cried when the unicorn turned to look at her. She froze, not wanting to scare him off.

The unicorn curled his lips to taste the cool air. Maggie stepped backward as he began to cross the stream and walk toward her. Because she wasn't paying attention to what was behind her, she tripped and landed sitting down.

When hot breath tickled the top of Maggie's head, she looked up. The unicorn was standing directly over her. She was too afraid to move as he knelt down and placed his head in her lap. Seeing prickers in his mane, she forgot to be afraid. Maggie gently pulled them out one by one. The unicorn seemed grateful and turned his head so she could reach all the prickers. When she was finished, he closed his eyes and relaxed.

Maggie loved the quiet of the Enchanted Forest. She especially loved the magic creatures she saw there. This was the first time she had ever been so close to one, however. She was thrilled that she was actually touching a unicorn!

"Maggie, what's taking you so long?" shouted her stepbrother, Peter, from deeper in the woods.

At the sound of his loud voice,

4

the unicorn raised his head. When a twig snapped, the unicorn scrambled to his feet and galloped back across the stream.

A small triangle glittered in her lap. It sparkled bright white with hints of delicate blue and silver. Maggie had never seen anything like it!

Her stepbrother strolled down the path, waving a long stick. Maggie stuck the triangle in her pocket to look at later as he held up a broken bird's nest. "I knocked this out of a tree. Too bad there weren't any birds in it." He glanced at the bucket she'd left by the stream. "Mother's waiting for that water."

Maggie picked up her bucket and started toward the cottage. She longed to share her new treasure with a friend, but it wouldn't do any good to tell Peter about the unicorn. His mother, Zelia, had married Maggie's father only a few

months ago. Before the wedding, Zelia had lived in town with her husband and children. When her husband died, a friend had introduced her to Maggie's father. Neither Zelia nor her children had ever been in the Enchanted Forest before they moved there. No matter what Maggie said about magical creatures, her new family didn't believe her. Peter would just accuse her of lying again. Her father's new wife always took her own children's word over Maggie's.

Now that her father was off chopping wood on the far side of the forest, he would be gone for weeks. No one knew when he'd be back. It all depended on how long it would take for him to complete his job. And he'd had to go so deep in the forest that there was no way she could get a letter to him. Without her father there to stand up for her, Maggie felt more alone than ever. Talking about the magical unicorn would only get her into trouble.

9

Zelia was waiting outside when they reached the cottage. "You're late again!" she said. "Always dawdling and making up stories

to get out of work! Everyone in the family has jobs to do, and you never do yours the way you should. If you keep it up, I'm giving your bed to Peter. He does his work. He deserves a good night's rest. Don't let the family down again or Peter will get your bed. You'll sleep in the loft with the twins."

Peter grinned when he heard his mother.

"That isn't fair!" said Maggie. "My father built that bed for me!"

"Do your work and the bed will still be yours," said Zelia. "You can help Peter with the sheep today. Go on! No more of your dilly-dallying!"

# Chapter 2

An hour later, Peter herded the sheep down the path while Maggie followed slowly. He was carrying his long shepherd's crook. She was afraid that he might trip her with it, like he often did when she wasn't looking.

As they followed the path over a green-speckled hill, a branch broke in the forest with a loud *crack*!

"Baa!" cried the sheep as they scattered. Peter ran after them, shouting.

A curious young griffin flew out of the forest and started to follow the sheep. Maggie ran toward the griffin. She waved her arms in the air.

"Shoo!" she whispered, trying

14

to warn it away. "I don't want you to get either of us in trouble!"

The griffin arched its neck and tried to peck her. Maggie picked up a small stone and threw it. The stone sailed past the griffin, who came after her again. The next stone grazed its wing. Startled, the griffin flew back into the forest.

By the time Maggie caught up with Peter, he had herded the sheep together again.

"Where have you been?" he asked. "Were you off looking for more imaginary animals? You should have been here helping me!"

"Sorry," said Maggie.

"You need to watch what's going on," Peter told her. "You're no use to anyone if you don't pay attention."

Maggie and Peter kept walking until they reached an open meadow. Peter stopped to let the sheep graze. He pulled out his reed flute and began to play. Lilting notes filled the meadow, calming the sheep.

Maggie waded through the tall grass until she found a wild raspberry bush growing at the edge of the woods. She plucked some berries and popped them

into her mouth. When she bit down, the sweet juice exploded on her tongue. Maybe tending sheep wouldn't be so bad after all.

Maggie was reaching for another berry when insects smaller than bumblebees swarmed out of the raspberry bush. Their wings made a faint whirring sound. One of them nipped her and she waved it away.

After a while, the sheep began to wander into the woods,

tempted by the cool shade and the tender leaves. Peter stopped playing his flute and jumped to his feet. "Don't just stand there!" he shouted. "Herd the sheep back here. Keep them out of the woods! I'll tell Mother if you don't!"

Maggie wanted to tell Peter how much she disliked him, or that he was an awful person, or that nobody liked tattletales. Instead, she squeezed her lips tightly together so she wouldn't say a word. Anything she said now would just make matters worse.

# Chapter 3

Maggie herded the sheep toward Peter. "I'll watch them from here," she said, keeping her distance.

"Fine," Peter grumbled. "We'll go to the meadow by the pond in a few hours." He sat down and started to play his flute again. While the sheep were happily munching grass, Maggie picked wild daisies.

She had a wonderful idea! She would make a beautiful daisy crown for her new unicorn friend. When she had enough flowers, Maggie sat on a rock and began making the chain. It didn't take her long to finish. Examining her handiwork, she wondered if the unicorn would like it.

As the day grew hot, the sheep lay down for naps. Peter stopped playing his flute. Maggie settled back to watch the high, puffy clouds. She saw a bunny with big ears and a castle with tall towers. Maggie watched the

clouds float by and rested her eyes for just a moment . . .

Suddenly, she was startled by the laughter of goblins. She listened closely then, but all she could hear were the birds singing in the trees and the bees buzzing around the wildflowers. Thinking that she must have imagined it, she closed her eyes. The goblins' laughter rang out, louder than before.

Maggie sat up. The goblin laughter had been real! She turned to

warn Peter that the sheep were in danger, but he was gone. The sheep were gone, too, luckily.

The laughter grew louder. The goblins had almost reached the meadow. There wasn't time to run away. They'd see her before she reached the path. Most goblins weren't smart, but they were fast. If she ran, they were sure to catch her. Maggie had only one choice. She'd hide in the tall grass and hope they didn't see her.

26

Maggie threw herself onto the ground. She could hear the goblins talking now. Worse, she could smell them. Goblins were extra stinky.

"You took my squirrel! I hungry!" shouted one goblin.

"You ate my rats!" cried another. "That squirrel mine!"

"Snickle, Geebo, be quiet!" shouted a third voice. "I hungry for tasty sheep! I hungry for tasty shepherdess! They gone now! You

27

noisies scare sheep away! I still hungry! That squirrel mine!"

The goblins shoved and pushed each other. They fell down with a thud and rolled around on the ground. Maggie could hear them grunting. If they came any closer, they might roll right over her!

Maggie held her breath. The goblin smell was strong enough to make her nose burn and her eyes water.

An ant walked across Maggie's cheek and she squeezed her eyes

shut. When something tickled her arm, she tried not to move.

The goblins were knocking each other around the meadow when something bit Maggie's wrist. Her eyes flew open. A tiny horse had landed on her. It was smaller than a bumblebee, but had wings like a butterfly and hooves as small as the heads of pins.

Soon, an entire herd of little horses landed on Maggie. Some nipped her with their tiny teeth.

Others kicked her with their tiny hooves. Maggie bit her lip. She didn't want the goblins to hear her.

One tiny horse landed on her ear and stomped its feet, tickling her. Without thinking, she moved her hand just enough to brush it off. The tiny horse fell to the ground and looked up at her with terrified eyes.

One of its wings was broken!

Maggie gasped when she realized what she'd done. She felt awful.

She hadn't meant to hurt the little horse! Now she'd have to help it, but she wasn't sure how. And the goblins were getting closer!

# Chapter 4

The sudden thundering sound of full-size hooves made the goblins stop fighting. Shrieking, they ran from the meadow. Maggie raised her head and peeked over the grass. The silver unicorn had returned and was chasing the goblins! Her new friend had saved her.

Maggie was safe. For now, at least.

When Maggie sat up, the little horses flew away. Only the one with the broken wing stayed behind.

Maggie was gentle when she picked up the tiny horse. Frightened, it reared and struck out with its hooves. Maggie cupped her hands around it.

She wished she could fix the broken wing herself. If only she knew how! She couldn't take the horse home. Her stepmother and stepbrother would only cause it more harm.

"I think I might know of someone who can fix your wing," she told the tiny horse.

Maggie's grandmother had told her lots of stories when she was younger. Some had been about a man who took care of magical creatures and lived in a stable just outside the castle walls. His name was Bob the Stableman. Maggie wasn't ever sure if the stories were true or not—she had been too young to find out on her own. But right now, more than ever, she hoped her grandmother's tales were true. She was going to take the tiny horse to see Bob.

Maggie looked at the sky. The sun was high overhead, which

meant it was lunchtime. Peter would be angry again because she hadn't followed him to the meadow by the pond. His mother would be furious, too. She would give Maggie's bed to Peter. Tears pricked Maggie's eyes when she thought about her bed. She tried not to think of Peter or her step-mother. This tiny horse needed her help.

Although Maggie knew the way to the castle, she had never gone by herself before. Her father had always taken her to the festivals held on the castle grounds. One of her earliest memories was of riding on his shoulders as they approached the gates. Her father was tall and the gates didn't seem quite so big. Nothing was as scary when her father was around. She missed him very much and wished that he were here now!

Maggie sighed and checked the tiny horse one last time. Then,

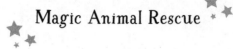

determined to be brave, she held
her head high and started walking.

# Chapter 5

Maggie walked very quietly on the path through the Enchanted Forest. She had to see what was happening around her. She had to listen in case something was coming her way.

Her eyes darted from side to side as she walked along the path. She spotted fairies swinging from long willow leaves. They giggled when they saw her and waved hello. She waved back and the fairies giggled even louder.

Maggie was passing a stream when she noticed a fawn and its mother drinking at the water's edge. She slowed to watch them and a voice called out to her. "Are you a princess in disguise by any chance?"

Maggie looked around, but didn't see anyone. She thought she might have imagined it until the voice called, "I'm down here!"

When Maggie looked down, she saw a frog gazing up at her. She took a step closer to get a better look. Was her mind playing tricks on her? Had a frog really just waved?

"It's rude to stare," said the frog. "Answer my question. Are you a princess or not?"

43

Maggie shook her head. "No, I'm not. Why do you ask?"

The frog sighed. "I'm a prince and I need a princess to kiss me."

"I didn't know that frogs had princes and princesses," said Maggie.

"They don't," the frog snapped. "I'm a human prince. A wicked witch turned me into a frog, and I need a human princess to kiss me so I can become my old self again."

44

"I'm sorry. I'd love to help you, but I don't know any princesses," Maggie told him.

"Of course you don't," grumbled the frog. "No one who walks past here ever does."

Maggie started walking again. She saw a gnome polishing mushroom furniture, a tree nymph stepping out of a tree, and paw prints where a wolf had passed by. She finally reached the road leading to the castle.

45

After Maggie had been walking down the road only a few minutes, she heard crashing in the trees behind her. She stopped to look back. The trees were shaking as something big passed by. A troll stepped onto the road, coming her way. Maggie's heart began to beat faster. Trolls were even more dangerous than goblins! Her grandmother had told her that they were stronger and meaner and never gave up. They'd eat

anything, including a bear if they could catch one. But trolls also had poor eyesight and lousy hearing. Maybe it hadn't noticed her yet.

Maggie wondered if she should hide in the trees. She could wait for the troll to go past. But the troll spotted her. "I see food!" the troll shouted. "Stop, food!" The troll began to chase Maggie.

"I'm not your food!" Maggie shouted back. "Leave me alone!"

Maggie ran as fast as she could

47

with her cupped hand against her chest. She didn't want to drop the little horse.

Maggie ran until her legs grew tired. She ran until she thought she couldn't run another step. She still could hear the troll's big flat feet slap the ground. He was getting closer and closer.

*Boy, they can run for a very long time*, Maggie thought.

There had to be something else. Something that could help her.

48

She looked up to the highest branch, hoping for an idea, when she saw a glimmer of light through the treetops.

Sunlight! Trolls couldn't be out in the sun. Grandmother had said that it would turn them to stone.

There were so many trees in the Enchanted Forest that everything was in shade. But even a small patch of sunlight might help. All she had to do was keep going until she found one.

Maggie's breath was raspy when she finally saw the ruins of a building in a clearing. They were the remains of a small castle, built long ago. The walls had collapsed. The stones had fallen into jumbled piles. She could see rays of sunlight streaming through gaps in the trees.

Maggie headed for the ruins. She climbed the rocks to the closest patch of sunlight. It was hard to climb using only one hand.

The other hand still protected the tiny horse. She knew the troll was very strong and would catch up with her soon.

As quickly as possible, she scrambled to the top. The patch of sunlight was very small. If this didn't work, the troll would certainly catch her. She waited as the troll clawed his way up the stones. And then he was there, drooling as he stretched his arm toward her. The moment the

sunlight touched him, a flash of light nearly blinded Maggie. When she could see again, the troll was gray all over. He had turned into a solid block of stone!

Worried about the tiny horse, Maggie opened her hand a little and peeked inside. The tiny horse pawed and shook its head.

"Don't worry, little guy. We'll get you some help soon," Maggie assured it.

Climbing down using one hand

took longer than climbing up. Fear had made her stronger. Relief made her want to sit down and rest. Once she was on the road again, she glanced back at the ruins. The statue of a troll crowned the top now. It looked like it was reaching for something that wasn't there.

Maggie heard the sounds of the mill long before she saw it. She knew the miller and his son. For a second, she thought about stopping

to ask for help. But if she did, they would ask why she was alone and where she was going. They would take her back to her stepmother. They wouldn't understand about helping the tiny horse. Maggie walked quickly by the mill, hoping

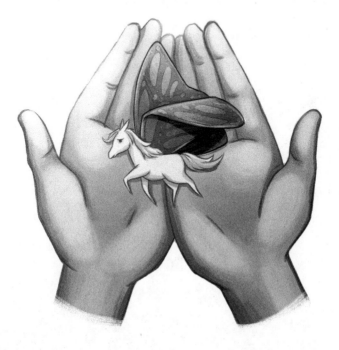

she wouldn't be spotted. Luckily, she didn't see either the miller or his son.

At the top of the next hill, Maggie saw the royal castle's tall towers. She was almost there! Now all she had to do was find the stable . . . and hope that Bob was real after all.

# Chapter 6

The road led straight to the castle's drawbridge. Maggie didn't want to go into the castle, so she turned onto a dirt path. Somewhere nearby there had to be a stable for magical animals. She was sure that her grandmother wouldn't have made up a story like that if there wasn't one.

Maggie passed a garden filled with blooming roses. Then, she passed a blacksmith shoeing a horse. She walked by a kennel where dogs barked at her. Neither the horse nor the dogs looked magical, though.

Finally, Maggie spotted an oddly shaped building. It looked like a cottage in the middle with two long buildings stuck on either end. Smoke came out of a chimney in the middle. Strange noises came from either end. Something growled. Something squawked. Something whinnied. Something bellowed. Something roared.

"Hold still so I can pick this stone out!" grumbled a man. "And stop leaning on me. I'm not your leaning post!"

Maggie crept to the door of the

stable and peeked inside. An old man was holding a white unicorn's hoof with one hand and using a tool to dig out a stone with the other. The unicorn snuffled the man's head. When the stone

popped out of the hoof, the man let go and stepped back.

The unicorn saw Maggie and nickered. The old man turned around.

"Who are you?" asked the man.

"I'm Maggie," she told him. "Are you Bob the Stableman?"

"I am," said the man. "Have you come to see me or my animals?" Taking the unicorn by its halter, he led it to a stall and shut the door.

"You," said Maggie. "I need your help. This little horse is hurt. See!" She held out her cupped hands and opened her fingers.

The man came closer to see what she held. "You caught a horsefly! That's very difficult. How did it get hurt?" he asked.

"I didn't mean to hurt it," said

Maggie. "It was tickling my ear and I brushed it off too hard, I guess. I walked a long way to bring it here. Can you help it?"

"Yes, but you'll have to leave the little horse with me," said the man. "I'll take good care of it for you."

"I feel awful about it," said Maggie.

"Don't be upset," replied Bob. "It's not your fault. The wings on tiny horses are very delicate and can break easily. It was good of you to bring it to me."

Maggie was relieved. After walking all that way, it would have been awful if Bob hadn't been able to help. She didn't feel quite so bad about the little horse now either, knowing that Bob would help it.

# Chapter 7

Maggie's eyes were wide and full of wonder as she looked around the stable. She'd never seen anything like it! So many magical animals in one place! If only her grandmother could have been there to see it. "Where will you keep the tiny horse?" asked Maggie.

"I have a special stall for little fellas just like him," said Bob. "I'll show you."

Maggie followed Bob into the stable and down a long hallway. There were enclosed spaces for magical animals on either side. Some of the stalls were big. Some were very small. They all had doors that were closed at the bottom and could open at the top. They were all tall enough for Bob

and Maggie to stand in. Maggie heard something grunt behind a closed door. She ran to take a look. She had to stand on tiptoe to see inside.

"What's that?" she asked, pointing at a pig. It had wings growing from its back.

"A flying pig, of course," said Bob.

She heard the mew of a kitten and ran to another stall. Opening the top door, she saw an animal in a box filled with straw, nursing its babies. They all had the long ears of rabbits and the long tails of cats. "What are they?" asked Maggie.

"Cabbits," said Bob. "A witch combined a cat and a rabbit. She thought they'd be extra cuddly. She was right."

When the mother cabbit started to get up, Bob quickly closed the door. "You can't keep their door open for long. They have the hind legs of rabbits and are very good jumpers."

69

Maggie followed Bob to a stall with moss on the floor and a puddle of water in the middle. A little tree grew beside the puddle. Tiny horses flew from the tree to the moss while others raced around the puddle.

"This is where your horsefly will live while he gets better," said Bob.

He showed her a tiny piece of wood the size of a splinter. "There are some nasty witches and some nice witches living in the

Enchanted Forest. I avoid the nasty ones, but most of the witches I've met are very nice. One of the nicest is a good friend of mine. She made this for me," he said.

Maggie opened her hands. Bob straightened the horse's wing and laid the tiny splint on top of it. The wood glowed. When it stopped glowing, it was stuck to the wing.

"The splint will fall off when the wing is healed," said Bob. "Why

71

don't you let him meet his new friends?"

Maggie stepped into the stall. She set the tiny horse on the moss. The horse bucked and galloped off. Other tiny horses followed him as he ran around the stall. Delighted, Maggie laughed. "I think he likes it here!"

"He'll be fine now," said Bob. "Once his wing is all better, you can help me let him go and return to his family."

"You mean I can come back?" Maggie asked, her eyes shining.

"You have to come check on him, don't you?" said Bob, smiling at her.

Maggie was thrilled! Here was someone she could talk to about magical animals who liked them as much as she did. And he'd actually invited her back!

Maggie and Bob left the stall. They closed the door behind them. Maggie was relieved that she'd found the magic stable. Her grandmother's stories had been true all along.

Standing side by side, they watched the tiny horses stop to smell each other, then race around the stall again.

"Why are his wings different from the others?" Maggie asked.

"Horseflies like these were made with magic," said Bob. He took a small book out of his shirt pocket. "Take a look at my record book. It's where I write down what I learn about all the magical animals I encounter."

"Your journal says that the horseflies live in tall grass," said Maggie. "That's where I hid from the goblins."

"You saw goblins!" exclaimed Bob. "That's not good! I'm glad you're all right."

"The goblins didn't see me in the grass," said Maggie. "But that's where the horseflies found me.

# A horsefly

Appearance:

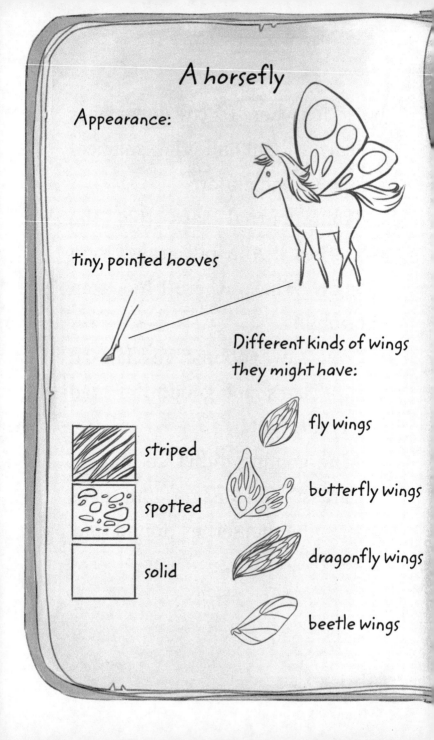

tiny, pointed hooves

striped

spotted

solid

Different kinds of wings
they might have:

fly wings

butterfly wings

dragonfly wings

beetle wings

Favorite foods: moss

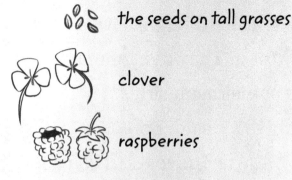

the seeds on tall grasses

clover

raspberries

Habitats: tall grass in meadows, mossy banks of streams, in fields of clover, in the mist of waterfalls, raspberry bushes

Sounds: faint whinny, faint nicker, faint neigh

Sleeping habits: usually standing up. Other times, some stand guard while others sleep lying down

Cleaning habits: gentle rain, mist of waterfalls

Other important details: the marks they leave when they bite (red mark with a purple center) or kick (tiny half-circle hoof mark) a human

Maybe they thought I was taking their food. They did get mad when I ate some raspberries."

"Maybe," said Bob. "Or maybe they were trying to warn you about the goblins. Horseflies are very brave creatures."

Maggie thought about that for a moment. She liked the idea of magical animals looking out for people.

"Hey, guess what! I also saw a griffin today," Maggie said. "Do you have anything in here about griffins?"

"As a matter of fact, I do," Bob said.

He opened the book to another page and handed it back to Maggie.

"The griffin I saw looked just like this picture!" said Maggie. "Did you draw it yourself?"

"I did," Bob told her. "Do you like to draw?"

Maggie nodded. "But I'm not as good as you are."

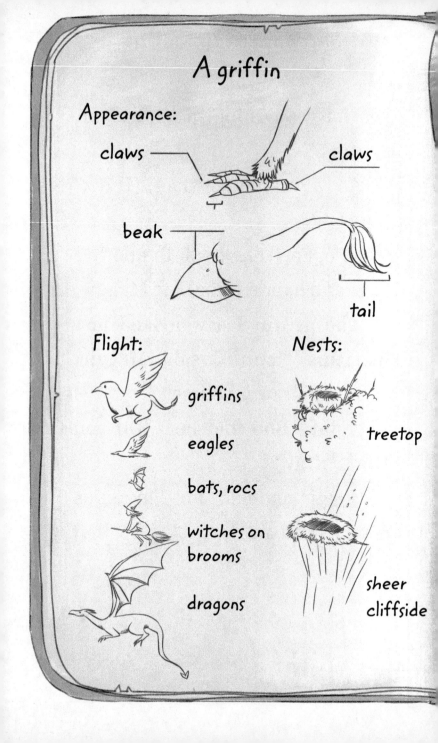

Wings:

hummingbird

owl

eagle

griffin

Where griffins most commonly found: forest, mountains

Sounds: screech when angry, clack of beak when curious, tut-tut sound when with young

Other important details: how to recognize a griffin when you are hiding in the dark—talons scraping, harsh squawk, shriek, clack of beak, stinky breath, brush of feathers

"I bet you could be if you practice," said Bob.

Maggie turned the page to read about another creature.

"You're right about trolls and sunlight," said Maggie. "The one that was chasing me today followed me up some rocks until a little patch of sunlight turned it to stone."

"A troll chased you and you got away! I'm so impressed with you, Maggie!" said Bob. "Very few people can escape from a troll."

Maggie smiled and blushed as she handed him the journal and he tucked it back in his pocket. "I add to the journal every time I find a new magical creature. Most people don't notice things like a horsefly. They think it's any old bug. They don't really *look* at it. You, however, see things that other people don't. Keep your eyes open. Let me know if you come across any more magical creatures."

# Trolls

Trolls are very persistent. If one is chasing you, do not stop until you get behind castle walls or run into a dragon. Trolls and dragons hate each other. If a troll sees a dragon, it will stop chasing you to pick a fight with the dragon.

Favorite food: anything except fruits and vegetables. They think humans are especially tasty.

Habitat: They sleep in caves and will not leave them on sunny days. If even a tiny bit of sunlight touches a troll, it will turn into stone.

Eyesight: extremely poor

Hearing: lousy, but not as bad as their eyesight

Sense of smell: good, but because they are so stinky, they can smell only themselves

To hide from a troll: Camouflage yourself with leaves or mud, stay far away, or hide behind a broad tree trunk. This works only if the troll has not already seen you. If a troll sees you—run!

"Really?!" Maggie exclaimed. "I'd like that. How long before my horsefly can fly again?"

"Probably two or three months," said Bob. "He'll need some time to properly heal. We should give him a name, don't you think? I've named all the other horseflies."

"I think I'll call him . . . Tickles," said Maggie. "I swatted him away because he tickled my ear."

Bob laughed. "That sounds like a good name. When he's all better,

we'll take him back to the meadow.
I'm sure he misses his family and
friends. While he's here, you
should visit him. Bring some grass
seeds or raspberries. He'll be eat-
ing out of your hand in no time."

"I will!" said Maggie.

She peeked into the stall again.
Maggie was glad she'd found
someone to help the horsefly, and
she couldn't wait to see even more
magical creatures!

# Chapter 8

Maggie watched the tiny horses play while Bob swept the floor where he'd cleaned the unicorn's hoof. She had been watching them for a while when Bob said, "I suppose you should be heading home. Your parents must be worried about you. I'll help you get there."

"You don't need to," said Maggie proudly. "I came here by myself. I know the way back."

Bob shook his head. "But that

wasn't safe. You ran into a troll on your way here. Who knows what you might meet if you walk back this late in the day."

"No one would have brought me," said Maggie. "My father is away at the other end of the forest chopping wood. He's been gone for days, and we don't know when he'll be back. My stepmother is busy with her children. They are all younger than me, except Peter, who's my age. He doesn't like me. Today he left me in the meadow by myself. That was right before the goblins came."

"You should never have been left alone. I want to meet your family," said Bob. "They need to know that Peter left you."

Maggie waited while he led an ordinary-looking horse out of a stall. "Why is he here?" she asked. "He doesn't look magical at all."

"You shouldn't judge someone by the way he looks," said the horse.

"You can talk!" said Maggie.

"So can you," the horse replied. "But I'm not making a big deal out of it."

"Maggie, this is Leonard," Bob said. "He's lived in the magic stable since he was a colt."

"Are we going to stand around talking or actually go somewhere?" asked Leonard.

"We're taking Maggie home," Bob said. He helped Maggie climb onto Leonard's back.

"Please don't tell my family about the horsefly," said Maggie. "They won't believe you if you do."

"I won't mention any magical creatures if you don't want me to," said Bob.

"I don't like the sound of these people already," Leonard muttered.

# Chapter 9

On the way to the cottage, Maggie did most of the talking. She told Bob about the griffin, the unicorn, and the goblins. She pointed out the troll statue. Bob was interested in all her stories. It was nice to talk to someone who really listened to

her and cared about what she had to say.

Suddenly, Leonard stopped walking and curled his lips. "What is it?" asked Bob.

"Goblins in the trees up ahead," said Leonard. "Can't you smell them? Should I outrun them? Or shall we show Maggie how you handle them?"

"Good idea, Leonard," Bob told him. "Maggie, you stay here. You'll be safe on Leonard's back."

Bob slid off the horse and walked a short way. Three goblins jumped out from behind the trees. They were the same three Maggie had seen that morning.

"Look what we find! Tasty treats!" cried the biggest goblin.

Bob pulled on the chain around his neck. When he held up his hand, something on the end of the chain flashed a bright white light. The goblins ran away, screeching.

Bob chuckled as he climbed onto Leonard's back again.

"What did you show them?" asked Maggie.

Bob handed the chain to Maggie. A glittery triangle dangled from the chain. "It's the tip of a unicorn's horn," he said. "They break off now and then. I find them in the unicorns' stalls sometimes."

Maggie looked worried.

"Don't worry, the tips always grow back," Bob reassured her.

"Goblins will see that piece of horn and run for the hills."

Maggie handed the chain back to him and pulled her own glittery triangle from her pocket. "I found one this morning just like that. See? But I didn't know what it was. Why are goblins so afraid of unicorns?"

"Unicorns can get rid of poison with the touch of their horns," said Bob. "Goblin blood is half poison. If a unicorn touches a goblin with

its horn, the goblin will disappear—
*poof!* Like that! Those little pieces
of unicorn horn are good protec-
tion," said Bob. "Don't ever leave
home without one!"

Maggie nodded and clutched
the tip of her
unicorn horn
just a little
tighter.

# Chapter 10

Maggie loved riding on Leonard's back. She had never ridden a horse before and was surprised by how quickly they reached the path that led to her family's cottage. It was late afternoon when they spotted

the little building with the thatched roof. The yard was full of children playing. Zelia stormed out the door as Bob helped Maggie get down from the horse.

"Where have you been?" Zelia shouted at Maggie. "Peter said he had to watch the sheep all by himself today."

"Actually, your son left Maggie in the meadow," said Bob. "He should never have done that! Something terrible could have happened!"

"And who are *you*?" Maggie's stepmother demanded.

"The Royal Stable Master and Keeper of Strange Creatures," said Bob. "You can call me Master Bob. Maggie is a friend of mine and may visit me whenever she wants.

She's going to help me with important work."

"What if I need her here? She's got important work to do at home, too," said her stepmother.

"Of course. Maggie can help you for part of the day, and then help me after," said Bob. He turned to face Maggie. "I hope to see you soon."

"You will! I promise," said Maggie.

"If she doesn't show up, I'll come

get her myself," said Leonard. "These people are worse than I thought!"

Maggie saw the surprised look on her stepmother's face. The other children seemed just as surprised. They'd actually seen—and *heard*—a talking horse. Maybe now they'd start believing her! But a moment later they acted as if nothing had happened. Maggie couldn't believe they were going to ignore something they'd seen for themselves!

"You didn't do your job today," said Peter. "What's it like to lose your bed?"

Maggie stuck her face close to his and said, "I'm not afraid of you. If I can handle goblins, I can handle a scrawny boy!"

"Goblins?" said Peter. He sounded as if he didn't believe her and rolled his eyes.

"That's right," Maggie replied. "There are all sorts of creatures in this forest. You need to pay more attention!"

"Maggie, I have something for you," said Bob. He handed her a journal and a pen. The journal was just like the one he'd shown her at his stable. "This is yours now. If anyone takes it from you, I will be

very angry. I put a spell on it, so I'll know who took it." He gave Peter a stern look, then turned and winked at Maggie.

Maggie smiled when she saw the look on Peter's face. Her step-brother didn't know that Bob's threat wasn't real. Bob's wink had told her one thing; he didn't have magic any more than she did. But it was a great threat, especially if Peter believed it.

When Maggie ran her fingers

over the cover of the journal, her smile got even bigger. No one had ever given her anything like this before. She was already in love with it.

"Write in it every time you see something unusual or magical. Write down any details you notice. Practice your drawing, too! Always keep this journal with you. You never know when you'll see something worth noting. Start with the creatures you saw today.

111

I'd especially make note of that troll."

"You saw a goblin *and* a troll in the same day?" Peter said, looking doubtful.

Bob ignored Peter and turned to Maggie. "Keep good notes. We're bound to notice different things, but this way we can learn from each other!"

"I'd like that," said Maggie. "There are so many things I want to learn about the magical

112

creatures in the forest. Oh! I know just what I want to write about first!"

Maggie turned to the opening page of her new journal.

My new friend, she wrote.

Bob smiled as Maggie drew a picture of him.

# About the Author

E. D. Baker is the author of the Tales of the Frog Princess series, the Wide-Awake Princess series, the Fairy-Tale Matchmaker series, and many other delightful books for young readers, including *A Question of Magic*,

*Fairy Wings*, and *Fairy Lies*. Her first book, *The Frog Princess*, was the inspiration for Disney's hit movie *The Princess and the Frog*. She lives with her family and their many animals in rural Maryland.

www.talesofedbaker.com